Henry The Ladybug

Written by Nancy Pulling Best
Illustrated by Mathew S. Capron

Henry The Ladybug

by Nancy Pulling Best

June 2019

Illustrations and Illustration Editing by Mathew S. Capron
Raleigh, North Carolina

Published by
Petrie Press
A Division of Nancy Did It
2985 Powell Road
Blossvale NY 13308
www.nancydidit.com

Printed in the United States of America

ISBN 978-0-9711638-9-8

Dedications

This book is dedicated to my mother, Betty Pulling. She loved to read to me and when my kids came along, she loved to read to them, too. She had a book of 100 poems that I loved. I credit her with my love of poetry both reading and writing.

Nancy Pulling Best

Scottie, Mom, Kelly

To my daughter who will always be my inspiration to enjoy life to the fullest. Also to the rest of my family for teaching me the ability to laugh at most things that come my way, appropriate or not...

Mathew S. Capron

Henry was a ladybug
he had seven spots.

Henry and his wife had kids, they had lots and lots and lots.

With so very many kids, the work was never done.

Food was always needed, they ate more than a ton.

Aphids were a favorite so Henry built a luncheon stand.

APHIDS!

POP
APHI

He sold all kinds of aphids like mashed and fried and canned.

Henry could make smelly stuff that came out of his knees.

When something tried to hurt him, he'd smell so bad they'd flee.

When a toad would come along instead of feeling dread,

the ladybug would just lay down, be still and he'd play dead.

One day NASA came to town to get bugs who were in shape.

They wanted them to go to space to see if aphids could escape.

They took Henry to Florida. He had to do some training.

The shuttle crew was ready to take off even though it was raining.

They also took some aphids for a zero gravity test.

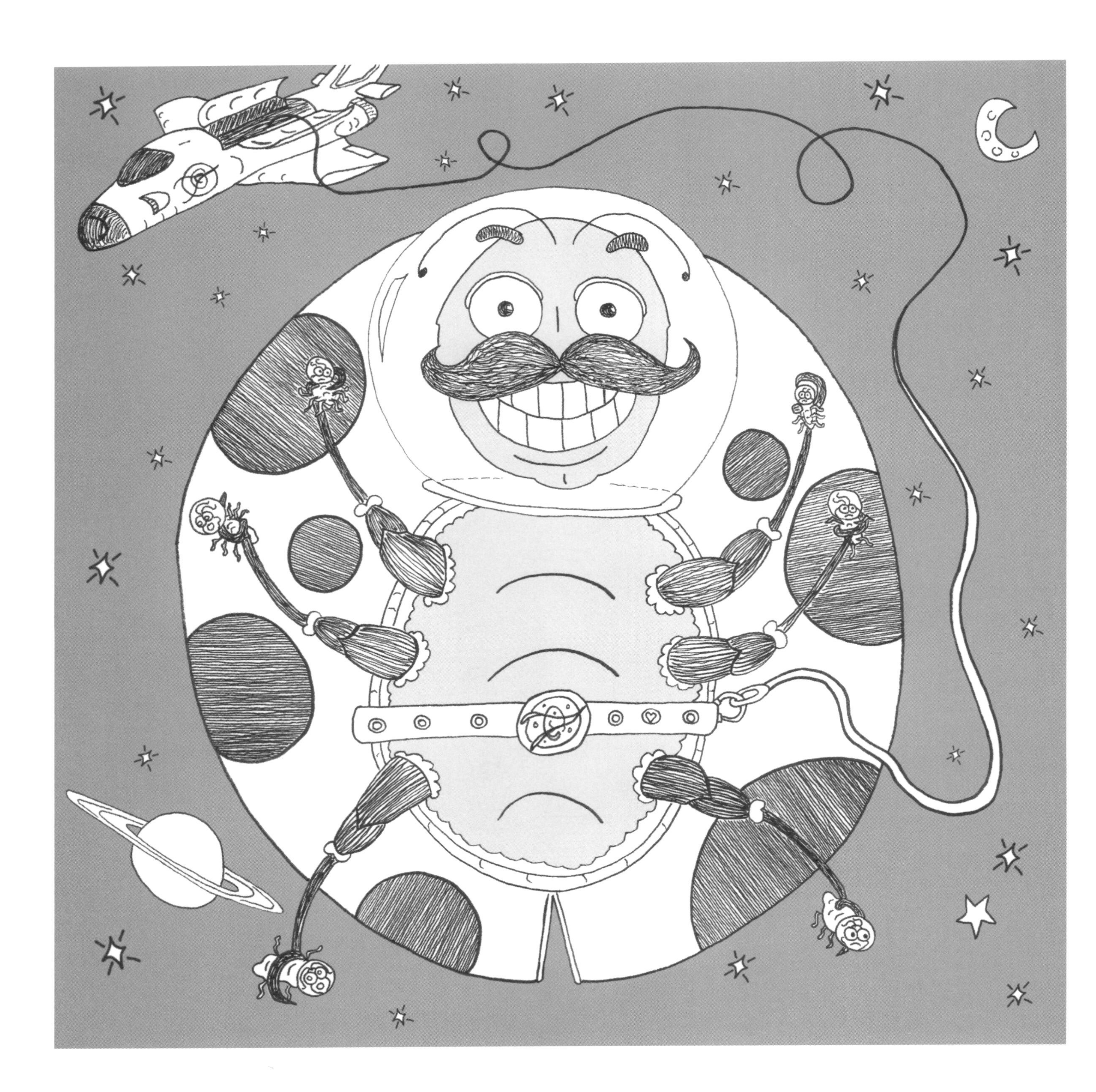

But Henry still could catch them all and proved he was the best.

Lady Bugs Really

For years scientists have known that lady-bugs will climb a stalk to capture aphids and aphids will escape by falling off the stalk with the help of gravity.

The burning question that still remained was how would the aphid's defense mechanisms work in the absence of gravity? In other words, what would the aphid do to escape the ladybug in space?

Finally, in 1999 four ladybugs were sent into

Did Go To Space!

space on NASA's space shuttle led by Eileen Collins. Ladybugs and their favorite food, aphids, were sent to zero gravity to study how aphids would get away without the aid of gravity.

After completing the mission, it was evident that ladybugs survived and did eat aphids in a microgravity environment.

Seems like ladybugs could qualify being astronauts!

Meet The Author: Nancy Pulling Best

Born and raised in the Adirondack mountains in upstate New York, Nancy prides herself in being a 4th generation Adirondacker.

"My great grandparents, grandparents, parents, children and 1st grandchild were all from the Old Forge, area in the Adirondacks," Best said.

After writing for her own personal use, newspapers and magazines, she brings you her fifth children's book.

She also authored "Anna the Spider," "Pepper the Dragonfly," "Bob the Bumblebee," "Lily The Grasshopper," "Learning To Cook Adirondack" and "Learning To Cook Adirondack Over An Open Fire." They are all available at www.nancydidit.com

Meet The Illustrator: Mathew S. Capron

Born and raised in the Adirondack mountains in upstate New York and now residing in the Carolinas, Mat always had a love for art and found a lot of peace in it.

He is the father of a beautiful daughter, who also enjoys being creative.

"I'm happy to have had an opportunity to illustrate this book," Mat said. "I hope you find happiness and peace within."

Mat also illustrated "Anna The Spider" "Pepper The Dragonfly," "Bob the Bumblebee." and "Lily The Grasshopper." More art and illustrations by M@ can be found at... hew-Art.com

Henry has lots of bug friends...
Be sure to check out their
adventures too!

Mapron